The Gotcha Plot

by Margo Sorenson

For Jim, Jane, and Jill, who never let me get too serious.

M. S.

Cover Illustration: Doug Knutson
Inside Illustration: Michael A. Aspengren

13 14 15 16 17 18 PP 12 11 10 09 08 07

For information, contact
Perfection Learning® Corporation
1000 North Second Avenue, P.O. Box 500
Logan, Iowa 51546-1099.
Phone: 1-800-831-4190 • Fax: 1-800-543-2745
perfectionlearning.com
48532
PB ISBN-13: 978-0-7891-0234-8
PB ISBN-10: 0-7891-0234-X
RLB ISBN-13: 978-0-7807-5515-4
RLB ISBN-10: 0-7807-5515-4

Contents

1

Targets!

Cecil stared straight ahead. The school door loomed in front of him. He tried to ignore them. But their voices behind him rang in his ears.

"Who's the loser?"

"Look at those glasses, will ya? They must be three inches thick!"

"Hike yer pants up higher, bud!"

"It's a geek! A real live geek! Who let him out of the zoo?"

Who were these guys anyway? Why couldn't they leave him alone? He couldn't help it if he wore thick glasses. He couldn't help it if he looked like the "before" in the weight-training ads. Cecil sighed. Being in a new school was so hard.

Cecil entered the school just as the bell rang. As he turned to his left, he took a chance and glanced behind him. He saw two boys swagger away to the right. One was huge. One was smaller.

What a joke, Cecil thought. The small one was trying to copy the big one's actions. It looked stupid.

If only he could have said what he was thinking. Ignoring them was so tough. Cecil looked at his spindly arms and sighed. He had no choice but to pretend he didn't care. Then finally, they'd probably leave him alone.

That's what had happened in his other schools. He'd just have to wait them out. Be patient. Pretty soon they'd get tired of teasing him and leave him alone.

His Uncle Wallace kept telling him he'd grow. "Hang in there," Uncle Wallace would say. "Until then, just ignore 'em." But it was so hard to take the hassling in the meantime. It made him feel like even more of a loser.

Cecil pulled out his crumpled class schedule. He studied it for the hundredth time. Then he looked up. Yes. Room 212. He was in the right place.

But no one else was heading into room 212. He checked his schedule again. It said 212.

All around him, students were running through the halls. They all seemed to be going the same way. What did they know that he didn't? His stomach tightened.

"We'll be late for assembly!" he heard one girl yell.

Assembly? Oh, so that was why no one was in class. There was an assembly first. Cecil frowned. Why hadn't the counselor told him?

He hitched up his backpack and followed the surge of bodies. Up ahead was a set of double doors. Above the doors he read "Meehan Auditorium."

He walked in. A wave of sound hit him. Everywhere students were yelling to each other.

"Cassandra! Save me a seat!"

"Not *there,* you idiot!"

"Oh, no! Mather for English!"

"Song! Song! Over here!" A loud chorus of boys' voices made Cecil turn his head. A large boy headed toward the guys who had been calling. They were motioning for him to join them.

Cecil sighed. No one would be calling out *his* name. He'd be sitting by himself.

Cecil scanned the seats closest to him. There! Right next to some girl. She looked harmless. He dropped down thankfully into the seat. Good thing he hadn't come in late. Everyone would have stared. They would have laughed. He didn't need any more problems. He just wanted to be unnoticed—invisible.

Cecil looked up at the stage. It was brightly lit. A

banner hung above. "John F. Kennedy Middle School" it read.

Familiar voices broke into his thoughts.

"Lookit the shrimp!"

"Hey! This isn't the elementary school!"

"Did your widdo mommy forget your widdo vitamins? Is that why you're a midget?"

He knew the voices. The same guys who had called him a geek. Cecil looked around. He saw the two sitting three rows ahead. And this time they weren't talking about him. They were pointing and laughing at someone else.

Cecil raised himself up in his seat to see. The guy they were picking on *was* pretty short. And boy did he look mad. Cecil strained his ears to hear.

"You wanna make something of it?" the short kid yelled. His fists were doubled. Cecil's eyes widened. All right! A fight!

Just then, a teacher walked up. She looked at the short angry kid with his fists up.

"Sit down," the woman said. Then she turned to the large boy. His buddy, the smaller one, backed away, trying to look innocent. He looked scared too.

The teacher glared at the bigger boy. "I've talked to you jokers about this before. Haven't I?" she growled.

"Yes, ma'am, Mrs. Harvey," the small boy answered quickly. "We're sorry, ma'am. We really are. We didn't mean anything. Honest." He smiled a big fake smile.

What a jerk, Cecil thought. And what a phony.

"Now find a seat. And keep your mouths shut," the teacher barked.

When the teacher looked away, the large boy rolled his eyes. Then the two quickly slunk off to another part of the auditorium.

Huh, Cecil thought. So those two jokers must do that all the time. They must make a career of hassling people. He hated guys like that. And the smaller one was such a phony!

Cecil hoped he wouldn't have either of them in his classes. Sure, he could probably handle their rude comments until they got tired of him. He'd done it before. But it sure wouldn't be any fun. He sighed.

"All rise for the pledge to the flag!" said Mrs. Harvey. She was up on the stage now.

Everyone stood up. They mumbled the pledge and sat down. Cecil listened during the assembly. He had to figure out what was going on at this school.

Mrs. Harvey introduced herself. She was the vice-principal. Then Mrs. Lawler introduced herself as the principal. She talked on and on.

Cecil snorted. These teacher-types always thought they were giving you something new and different. Always the same stuff. Always. "Work hard. Be respectful of others." Blah, blah, blah. He had to admit that those two bullies could use the "be respectful" junk.

Finally, the assembly was over. "You are dismissed to

your homeroom classes," Mrs. Lawler said.

Students pushed and shoved through the doors. Their loud voices filled the hallways.

Cecil walked quickly through the halls to room 212, his homeroom class. He hoped he'd have a decent homeroom. After all, he'd have to see these kids every morning. And every afternoon. All year long. He was nervous as he walked through the door.

The first person he saw was Song. He was seated. Another boy was leaning on Song's desk, talking to him and smiling.

Cecil looked around. There was the hot-tempered short guy who'd been hassled at the assembly. Even now, he still looked mad. Cecil felt they had something in common.

Cecil dropped down into the next desk. He decided to start a conversation. He could use a friend or two.

"Hey," he said to the boy. "My name's Cecil. I'm new here." He grinned. "I saw what happened in assembly this morning. They hassled me too."

The boy turned and looked at him. He looked surprised. "Hi," he said slowly. "I'm Carlos. I'm new too." He frowned. "There sure are some jerks at this school."

"Uh-huh," Cecil said. "I..."

A voice broke in. "Look! It's the shrimp and the nerd!"

"Yeah, they're making friends! Awwww! How cute!"

Cecil's heart sank to his shoe tops. No! It couldn't be. He turned around. It was. His worst fears were coming true. Behind his row of desks stood the same two guys from this morning.

"Oh great," Cecil muttered. He sighed and slid down in his desk. Then he looked at Carlos. Carlos was scrambling out of his desk.

"You—" Carlos spluttered. His fists were clenched.

Quickly, Cecil reached out a hand. He pulled Carlos back down. "Hey, man," he said in a low voice. "Calm down."

"Boys! Boys! Please!" a teacher's voice called weakly.

Cecil looked up. Was this his homeroom teacher? Was this the teacher who was supposed to keep order? No way.

"I—I'm your teacher, Miss Reed," she said. She cleared her throat. "Let's all settle down. You'll have to help me out. I'm new to the school."

Terrific. She was little and blonde. She looked about twelve years old. Even from where he sat, Cecil could see her hands trembling. She looked nice. But she wasn't going to have any control. He could already see that.

He and Carlos looked at each other. They rolled their eyes. Then they grinned.

Miss Reed began calling roll. "Please sit alphabetically." Her voice wavered.

Cecil jumped up when she called "Cecil Besser." He

took his seat near the back of the first row.

"Carlos Bixby," Miss Reed called next.

Good, Cecil thought. He and Carlos grinned at each other.

Miss Reed kept calling names. Cecil listened and watched. He wanted to know what the two jokers' names were.

"Hendry Lawson," Miss Reed called.

The huge one sauntered to his desk. When roll call was finished, Cecil had the other guy's name too. The phony little guy was Reno Wilkins. All the rest of the names were a blur.

Reno had strutted to his desk too. Just like Hendry. The two of them acted as if they owned the school.

Cecil almost moaned aloud. Every day, twice a day, he would have to see them. Luckily, they were sitting on the other side of the room.

The bell rang. "Oh no!" Miss Reed wailed. "I didn't finish half of what I had to do!"

Poor Miss Reed, Cecil thought. Kids were already rushing for the door. Cecil and Carlos stood up to walk out together.

"Hey, isn't there a midget exit?" Hendry called. He shoved into Carlos. "And one for geeks too?" he added, shoving into Cecil. Cecil stiffened.

"Yeah! Yeah!" Reno said. His eyes gleamed.

Then Reno checked to see if Miss Reed was watching. Miss Reed was shuffling papers. She wasn't even looking up.

"A geek and midget entrance! We could make a small sign," Reno cackled. "Get it? A midget sign for midgets!" He looked at Hendry eagerly. Reno was a real loser.

Then Cecil noticed Carlos' eyes narrowing. He grabbed Carlos' arm and pulled him back.

"Let 'em go," Cecil hissed. "We'll handle them later. Let's just get to class."

Carlos jerked his arm away. "All *right,*" he groused. "You're not my mother," he complained.

"No, but looks like you could use one," Cecil joked. "You're gonna get your lights punched out. Settle down."

"They're idiots!" Carlos fumed. He stomped angrily down the hall next to Cecil.

"Uh-huh," Cecil agreed. "But that's not the way to stop them. They're a lot bigger than both of us." He looked at his skinny frame and sighed. This could be a long, long year in homeroom.

2

Target Practice Continues

At lunchtime, Carlos waited for Cecil in the hall. Their lockers were near each other's.

"Hey," Cecil said. He grinned. "You survived," he joked.

Carlos grinned back. "You made it too," he said. He took his lunch out of his locker and slammed it shut.

Cecil began twirling his combination lock.

"Hah! Did your mommy pack your widdo lunch?" Hendry's voice taunted from behind them. "Does she hope you'll grow?"

Cecil frowned. Weren't they going to get any breaks? He sensed Carlos stiffen next to him.

"Shut up," Cecil muttered through tight lips. "Don't say *anything*." He opened his locker.

"Check out the geek's locker. Ooooh—lookit the books!" Hendry crowed. "He must do his homework every night!"

Reno looked around quickly before speaking. "The loser must be a real student! Got a pocket computer, nerd?" he taunted.

Cecil grabbed his lunch from his locker.

Ka-bam! Before Cecil could stop him, Carlos shoved Reno right into the lockers.

"Unnnh!" Reno shouted. He looked surprised.

Carlos moved closer to Reno. His fist was up.

"Hey, midget," Hendry said threateningly. He took a few steps forward. He shook his fist in Carlos' face.

Hendry's warning sure didn't seem to bother Carlos, though. Carlos just squared his shoulders.

"Wanna make somethin' of it?" Carlos asked. He jutted his chin in the air.

"All right, boys," an adult voice called. "Knock it off."

Cecil looked over. It wasn't a teacher or Mrs. Harvey either. It must be the custodian. He held a sponge mop.

He wore blue work pants. Cecil read "Custodial Staff" above the pocket of his blue work shirt. The man was glaring at Hendry and Reno.

Hendry gave the custodian a hard look. But he nodded to Reno. "Let's go," he said. "Before Mr. O'Malley douses us with chemicals," he snapped.

"Everything's cool, Mr. O'Malley. Honest," Reno said quickly. He gave a fake smile. "Have a nice day," he added.

Then he and Hendry walked quickly down the hall. Before they walked through the doors, Hendry turned around. He gave Cecil and Carlos a long, hard look.

Cecil felt a little shiver run from his scalp to his toes. Hendry was mean. He could see that. But at least he wasn't a faker like that Reno.

Cecil turned to the custodian. "Uh, thanks," he said.

"No problem," the man said. "I'm Mr. O'Malley. Your helpful custodian," he added, grinning. "I try to clean up the school." He jerked his thumb in the direction of the exit.

Cecil glanced down the hall. Reno's and Hendry's backs were disappearing. Cecil grinned. "Yeah," he said. "They need cleaning up." He shut his locker.

"You two are new here, right?" Mr. O'Malley asked.

Cecil and Carlos nodded.

"Well, they're not," he said. He nodded his head in the direction of the two boys. "I know 'em better than I want to. They're trouble for everyone around here. They think they run the school. There are just a few kids who can face them down."

Mr. O'Malley shook his head. "Mrs. Harvey does keep them in line. But it's almost always *after* something's happened. Not before." He grinned at Cecil and Carlos. "You two ever need any help, just ask," he said.

"Thanks," Cecil said. He elbowed Carlos.

"Uh, yeah, thanks," Carlos added.

"No problem," Mr. O'Malley said.

Mr. O'Malley walked down the hall. He opened a door labeled "Custodian." He seemed okay. And he sure was better than Miss Reed. Cecil snorted. Mr. O'Malley could handle punks. Miss Reed just wilted. Poor Miss Reed.

Cecil and Carlos walked out into the quad. They squinted in the bright sunshine. Dozens of students sat on the grass, eating lunch. Some sat at tables. Cecil and Carlos looked at each other.

Carlos nodded his head over at an empty space on the grass. Cecil looked around carefully. Hendry and Reno were nowhere in sight.

"Sure," Cecil said. Together, they walked over to the spot. They dropped down on the grass.

All around him, Cecil heard students' voices. Laughter and loud chatter filled the air. He opened his soda. He gulped a few swallows. Then he set the open can down next to him.

Ka-wham! Cecil's soda can flew ten feet across the grass. Soda sprayed out everywhere. Kids started yelling and calling out.

"Hey!" Cecil yelled. He looked up into the face of guess who?

"Oh, so sorry," Hendry sneered. "Me and my friend were just doing a little kicking practice." He turned to grin at Reno. Reno hung back, smirking. "Guess your soda can got in the way." Then they both laughed.

"Yeah," echoed Reno. He looked around and saw everyone watching. He puffed out his chest. "Sorry about that."

They turned to walk away. They were still laughing.

"You losers try that again, you're gonna have a problem," a voice called out next to them.

Cecil blinked. He looked over. Song was glaring at the two boys.

Hendry and Reno stopped and turned around. They looked worried.

Song would be a good person to know. Maybe he was one of the kids Mr. O'Malley was talking about. The kids who could handle the two jerks.

"Ah, sure, Song," Reno said quickly. "It was an accident." He smiled the fake smile again. "They left their stuff right in the way."

Carlos hopped up. "That was no accident!" he bellowed.

Cecil grabbed Carlos' arm and pulled him down. "They'll chew you up and have you for lunch."

Reno and Hendry shuffled away. They stopped under a tree, talking and laughing.

"Aaaah, those guys are losers," Song said in disgust. "They don't have anything better to do. So they go around acting like three-year-olds," he said.

Song grinned at Carlos and Cecil. "I'm Song. I'm in your homeroom. You're new to Kennedy, right?" he asked.

"Uh-huh," Carlos and Cecil said at the same time. They all laughed. They finished lunch together and got to know each other better.

After lunch, Cecil checked his schedule again. He didn't want to be late to any classes. Not the first day anyway. Right after lunch he went to history. He snoozed through that class. It was tough to stay awake in classes right after lunch. Thankfully, the troublemakers weren't in any of his classes.

Cecil opened the door to his math class. Carlos was right behind him. They had compared schedules at lunch and learned that they had math together.

"Look out! Nerd alert! Nerd alert!" Hendry's voice welcomed Cecil and Carlos. And there was his little shadow—Reno.

Cecil wanted to drop into a hole in the ground. Why him? Homeroom with these idiots was bad enough. They had to be in his math class too? There they were, grinning wickedly.

"Shrimp alert! Shrimp alert!" Hendry continued.

"A munchkin! It's a munchkin!" Reno said in a high-pitched voice. Some of the kids laughed. He turned around and smiled at them. "Munchkin! Munchkin!" he repeated.

"Can I borrow your pocket protector?" Reno asked.

"Shut up, you morons," a girl's voice said. Cecil stared. She was—well—definitely all right. He hid a smile. Math class might not be so bad after all.

Just then, Song walked in. As soon as he did, Hendry and Reno shut up. They got very busy with their books.

Cecil watched Song walk to his desk. Everyone seemed to want to say something to him. Voices greeted him from across the room.

"Hey, Song! Good game yesterday."

"Great touchdown!"

A shy grin spread across Song's face as he sat down.

The teacher blabbed for a while. But Cecil wasn't really listening. She stopped talking when a student walked into the room. She had a call slip from the office.

"Berneeta Williams?" the teacher asked. She looked around the class.

The girl who had told the jerks to be quiet raised her hand. "Yes'm?" she asked. "That's me."

"This message is for you. Your aunt is picking you up after school today," the teacher said.

From the next row, Cecil could hear Hendry whisper loudly to Reno.

"*I'd* like to pick her up after school," he said, grinning. "Can you still get us the office call slips to get out of class?" he asked. "Can you get one for me and her at the same time?"

"Shhhh!" Reno said in a low voice.

Reno looked around the classroom. Cecil pretended he was filling out his book card. This sounded interesting. He wanted to hear what Reno would say.

Next to him, he noticed Carlos' pencil stop moving. Carlos must be listening too.

"Yeah," Reno said softly. "I'll get a whole stack of call slips. Just like last year.

"I'll forge old Harvey's signature on them again," Reno went on whispering loudly. "Then when I'm office aide, I'll just drop them in the 'out' tray. They'll get delivered whenever you want." Reno snickered.

Whoa! Cecil thought. What a scam.

"All right, buddy," Hendry whispered. Then he leaned forward in his desk. He frowned. "What about Mrs. Harvey?" he asked. "What if you get caught?"

"I'm not afraid of Harvey," Reno bragged. "I can talk my way out of anything in this school!"

Oh yeah? Cecil sneered silently. Then why was Reno so scared of Mrs. Harvey in assembly? Reno must be all talk. He knew guys like that at his old school. They were real losers.

"Gentlemen? Let's pass in those book cards," the math teacher ordered.

Cecil looked over at Carlos. He wiggled his eyebrows. Carlos grinned back.

Okay, Cecil thought. Now they knew some stuff about these guys. Maybe that would help them.

3
Things Get Worse

The bell finally rang. Math class ended. Cecil and Carlos walked out of the room quickly.

"I can't believe you don't wanna fight 'em," Carlos complained. He stopped in front of their lockers.

"I *do,*" Cecil said. He looked at his arms and sighed. "I'd like to pound their faces into the ground. But they'd turn me into dog meat. And then the hassling just gets worse."

Cecil pulled books from his locker. "I learned patience the hard way at my last school." He made a face. "My uncle keeps reminding me. Just ignore them for now and wait, he says. Either they'll forget about you. Or you'll grow. And then you can take care of them." Cecil shrugged and zipped up his backpack.

They headed toward homeroom. Cecil was filled with dread. Homeroom would be the worst. Miss Reed had no control. Maybe after a while, the idiots would settle down. Maybe they were just like this the first days of school. Then he frowned. He remembered what Mr. O'Malley had said. "They think they run the school." It didn't sound like things would be getting better soon.

Cecil opened the door and walked in. Carlos followed him.

"Now, class," Miss Reed was pleading. "Please, class. Now, class." She looked worried.

Reno and Hendry were making spit wads. They hurled them at kids on the other side of the room. Song walked in. He looked around. Just then, a spit wad caught him on the ear.

"Hey!" he roared. He glared at Hendry and Reno. "Grow up!"

The class became silent. Cecil heard papers shuffling. A few kids whispered.

He and Carlos sat down quickly. Good thing they hadn't gotten to class earlier. The spit wads would have nailed them for sure.

"Thank you, Song," Miss Reed said. She looked as if she were about to cry. She shifted papers on her desk. "I—I can't seem to find my roll book," she said. She looked at the class. "Does anyone know where it is?"

Song got up. He walked over to Reno's desk and reached underneath. He held up a light green notebook. "Is this it, Miss Reed?" he asked. He gave Reno a disgusted look.

Reno pretended to look surprised. "What's that?" he asked in a fake tone. His eyes shifted from side to side.

"How did it get there?" Miss Reed asked. She looked around the class. Miss Reed frowned. "Did you take it?" she asked Reno.

Reno looked confused for a second. Then he looked really innocent. He opened his eyes wide. His voice went up. "Oh no, Miss Reed. I don't know how it got there," he lied.

What a cheat, Cecil thought. He looked over at Carlos. Carlos was shaking his head.

"Somebody else must have taken it," Reno went on. "Somebody wanted to get me in trouble," he whined. He looked slyly at Hendry. Then Reno pointed at Cecil.

"I bet he did it," he said, hiding a smile. Hendry snickered.

Cecil's back stiffened. Great! He was going to get in trouble for something he didn't even do! Wasn't Reno ever going to leave him alone?

"That's impossible," Miss Reed said, frowning. "He

just walked in."

Cecil felt a wave of relief wash over him. At least Miss Reed knew *some* things! From the corner of his eye, he saw Carlos grin at him.

Miss Reed sighed. She looked tired. "Besides, I'm not so sure that someone *else* took it." She frowned at Reno. "This better not happen again," she said.

"Forget it," Miss Reed sighed again. "Let's get started. I need to have you fill out these forms, please." She began handing out white cards to everyone. Cecil saw her hands tremble. Poor Miss Reed, he thought. She was trying so hard.

Cecil filled out his card. He sneaked a look at Reno. He was laughing and whispering with Hendry. This was just *one* day of school. How was he going to handle all the rest of the days?

The bell rang. "Hand in your forms, please." Miss Reed's voice echoed out into the hallway. Kids rushed for the doors without listening.

****

The next morning before school, Cecil shut his locker. Carlos hadn't shown up yet. Cecil hated the thought of facing homeroom without his one friend. He gripped the straps of his backpack. Well, if he had to, he would. He tightened his mouth. Maybe Song would be there. He seemed like a pretty good guy. And he sure didn't like Hendry and Reno.

THE GOTCHA PLOT

Cecil opened the door to homeroom. Miss Reed was writing stuff on the board. Kids talked and laughed with each other. He looked quickly at the other side of the room. Whew! The two idiots weren't there yet. Maybe they'd be sick. Maybe they got hit by a bus or something.

Cecil lowered himself into his desk. He unzipped his backpack. Had he put his English homework in his notebook last night? Why couldn't he remember?

Cecil's head bent over his three-ring binder. He leafed worriedly through the pages. Where was his grammar assignment? Where was it?

He had to find it. He didn't want to start out on the wrong foot. Then life just got harder. Teachers decided stuff about kids early. It was easier to start out well. Then if he messed up later, things weren't so bad.

Hah! There it was! He had put it behind the math divider. Stupid! Cecil opened the rings on his notebook. He'd move it to the right place. Carefully, he began to take the grammar homework page out. Ka-wham! His binder went flying through the air!

"Hey!" Cecil shouted. He jerked his head up.

His binder thudded on the floor. Because the rings were open, all his papers flew across the aisles. They drifted down like huge snowflakes. His pencils and pens rolled crazily across the floor. Kids stopped talking and stared.

"Oh! *Sorreeeee,*" Reno said, behind him. He grinned slyly at Hendry next to him.

Cecil jumped up. He could feel his anger rising. "Hey! What do you think you're doing?"

"It was an accident," Reno said, smirking. Cecil could hardly see through his haze of anger. Reno made his eyes bigger, trying to look innocent. "I kind of slipped."

Hendry snickered. Some kids in the classroom frowned. Some looked disgusted. Others began talking to each other again.

"It didn't look like much of an accident to me," Miss Reed said. She sounded mad. "I think you'd better watch it. The next stop is the vice-principal's office," she warned. Her voice shook a little.

Reno suddenly sobered. "I'm sorry, Miss Reed. It was an accident. I swear it. Here," he added, bending over. "I'll help clean up!"

Reno began to sweep the papers off the floor. He crumpled them as he handed them back to Cecil. He grinned slyly.

"Hey—I'll do my own stuff," Cecil said quickly. "Get outta the way." He pushed Reno aside. Reno stood up, smiling.

Cecil got down in the aisle and began picking up papers. Other kids helped. They passed papers down the aisle to him.

"Something like that better not happen again," Miss Reed warned. "Sit down everybody. Let's take roll," Miss Reed said. She frowned.

Cecil looked through the pile of dirty, messy papers on his desk and sighed. He hoped his English homework was okay. That wasn't going to impress his new teacher very much.

Cecil looked at his binder. The binder's spine had begun to rip apart from the fall on the floor. Great, he thought.

Cecil stared across the room at Reno and Hendry. Something was going to have to happen with those jerks. And soon.

4
Trapped!

"What a long week," Cecil remarked to Carlos, three days later. They walked into the quad together. "I feel like I've been at school a year."

"Me too," Carlos grumbled. "This has been the longest week of my life." He kicked a stone on the ground. It pinged into a metal trash can.

"I hate getting used to a new school," Cecil said. He hoisted his backpack up.

"You and me both," Carlos muttered. He kicked another stone. Thunk! It zipped into a tree trunk.

"And boy, that Hendry and Reno just don't let up," Cecil added. He looked around as he walked. Kids were talking and laughing. Some hurried across the grass to the main building.

Cecil grunted. "They hassle us before school. They hassle us during homeroom. At lunch. All during math class. After school. We get no peace," he complained. "And I'm getting tired of it," he added.

Cecil jumped up and pulled a leaf off a tree overhead. He flicked it into the air. It fluttered in the breeze.

"I'm gonna think of something to do about them," Cecil promised. "I don't know what yet, but I'll think of something. Maybe I'll try to talk to my Uncle Wallace.

"Reno's going to be the tough one," Cecil continued. "He's so sneaky." He sighed. "And this ignoring them stuff isn't doing much good."

The two boys walked into the hall. They stopped in front of their lockers. Cecil spun his lock. Carlos popped his locker open.

"Well, well. Look who's here." Hendry's voice rang in Cecil's ear.

Cecil jumped. Now what? he wondered. How much of this could he take? Maybe he should listen to Carlos. Sitting back and taking this abuse wasn't working.

"Yeah," Reno snickered. "It must be a geek convention," he said, trying to sound stupid.

Cecil didn't turn around. He stared into his locker. He could just see the smirk on Reno's face.

"The geek is loading up his homework for the weekend. Bet he can't wait to start studying," Reno sneered. "He likes to keep his papers all nice and neat in his notebook!" He laughed rudely. "He doesn't want to get the teachers mad! Oh, no! Can't do that!"

Cecil shut his eyes. Calm down, he told himself. Faced with these guys, he knew fighting back was not the answer.

Cecil glanced at Carlos. He'd been on Carlos all week to keep his mouth shut. From the corner of his eye, he could see Carlos jutting his chin out. Uh-oh. Trouble, Cecil thought.

"Sure!" Hendry's laughter jarred Cecil. "You know the nerd has nothing else to do. He has no *real* life."

"Hey," Reno's voice squawked. "Do you think nerds *always* hang around with midgets?" Then he cracked up. Hendry joined in with loud laughter.

Cecil wasn't sure how much more he could take. All he wanted to do was get out of there.

Suddenly, Carlos spun around. "Shut up, you idiots. At least we don't hang around with guys who have cottage cheese for brains! It's a good thing you've got muscles, cause your brains aren't gonna get you anywhere."

Then, before Cecil could stop him, Carlos shoved Hendry into the lockers. Hendry looked really surprised. He hadn't thought Carlos would cross him. But Carlos was much stronger than he looked. He was a wrestler and he lifted weights.

Hendry made a thud against the lockers that echoed down the hall. Kids stopped. They began to form a little circle around the four boys.

"Hey, Hendry," one voice taunted from the group surrounding them. "You gonna let him talk to you like that? A big dude like you?"

"Yeah!" another voice sneered. "Lookit the little guy get Hendry!"

Laughter followed.

Hendry rebounded off the lockers. His fists were doubled and his face was red with anger.

Cecil's heart pounded. Quickly, he looked for an escape route. He and Carlos had to get out of there. And fast!

But students blocked every way out. Everyone was whispering and muttering to each other. They were waiting to see the fight. There was no way to escape. He and Carlos were doomed. Where was Song when they needed him?

Reno hung back behind Hendry. He was hiding again. What a fraud Reno was.

Hendry walked toward Carlos. He grinned evilly. He flexed his fingers. This was the chance he had been waiting for.

"I think you guys need a lesson," he sneered. "You gotta be more polite. Come on, you puny, little runt," Hendry taunted. He began circling Carlos.

Carlos drew back his arm. Just as he was ready to throw a punch, Mrs. Harvey broke into the circle. Reno quickly jumped back into the crowd. He tried to hide.

Mrs. Harvey planted herself between Carlos and Cecil and Hendry. Her voice was like ice.

"I know what you're up to, Hendry," Mrs. Harvey said. "I know your style. Unless you want to get suspended, I suggest you hightail it out of here." Mrs. Harvey put her hands on her hips. She waited.

The group of students broke up. They began to move away slowly.

"Yeah. Okay," Hendry said sullenly. He squinted his eyes at Cecil and Carlos. He mouthed some words at them.

Cecil couldn't tell what he was saying. But he bet it wasn't "Have a good day."

Hendry thrust his shoulders back. He shoved his hands into his pockets. He tossed his head. Then he strutted away.

Reno copied Hendry's movements exactly. Cecil almost laughed out loud. Because Reno was so much smaller, he looked like a wind-up, miniature toy Hendry.

Mrs. Harvey watched them leave. She looked at Carlos and Cecil. She frowned. "I know you two are new to Kennedy. Try to stay away from those two.

"I know they work on your heads," Mrs. Harvey continued. "Just don't let them get to you. Because if you fight them, I have to haul *all* of you into the office." She grinned a half-grin. "And I have enough paperwork to do already. I don't need any suspension reports to fill out. Hear?"

"Yes, ma'am," Cecil said quickly. Mrs. Harvey was okay.

"Yeah," Carlos mumbled. He looked down at the floor. He was still very angry.

"All right, get on home. The show's over," Mrs. Harvey said to the last students staring at Carlos and Cecil.

As she walked off, Mrs. Harvey's footsteps echoed in the now-quiet hall. Cecil wiped the sweat from his forehead. Then he wiped his glasses. His hands still shook.

"Man!" he said to Carlos. "That was *close!*" He frowned. "I keep tellin' you—you gotta stay cool. Or else we'll be dog meat. Fighting isn't the answer." Cecil looked at his own skinny body and made a face.

"Well, standing around and doing nothing isn't the answer either," Carlos said. His face was shiny with sweat. *"They're* gonna be dog meat if they don't watch out."

"We don't stand a chance, and you know it," Cecil said. "And now they'll be looking everywhere for us." He put his glasses back on.

"You'll figure something out," Carlos said. He grinned at Cecil. "That's what friends are for. Right?"

The two boys slammed their lockers shut. They

walked down the hall and around the corner.

Cecil froze. Who was that at the end of the next hall? Two shapes lurked in the darkness. One big and one small. No. No. Not so soon. He swallowed hard.

"Uh, Carlos?" he whispered. He jerked his head in the direction of the shapes. "I—uh—think we better go another way," he said in a low voice. He hoped Carlos wouldn't want to take them both on. They'd be dead for sure.

Carlos' eyes narrowed. "Those jerks," he said. He tightened his mouth. He started toward them.

Cecil grabbed Carlos' shoulder. "No, man! Think! Everyone's gone. We'll get pounded. Let's go another way. We'll think of a way to get them back. I promise," he said earnestly.

Carlos stopped. "Yeah. I guess you're right. We'll make their heads spin."

Just as Carlos finished his words, Cecil saw the shapes advancing. His stomach was in a knot.

"Come on, let's hurry!" Cecil said. He took off down the hall toward their lockers. Carlos followed. Behind them, Cecil could hear tennis shoes pounding on the hall floor.

"Now look what you got us into!" Cecil panted. Sweat dripped onto his glasses. He reached up to wipe them off. "You and your big mouth!"

"Hey, man," Carlos said, running next to him. "I was just foolin' with 'em." He grinned. "You gotta admit. It was pretty good!" He slapped Cecil on the back. "Like that one about no brains and cottage cheese?"

"Hey! There they are! There are those losers!" a voice called from down the hall.

Cecil and Carlos raced around the corner to the hall where their lockers were.

Cecil froze. An exit was ahead of them at the other end of the hall. It read "Fire Exit Only—Alarm Will Sound."

"They're coming! What can we do now, Carlos?" he asked. His voice rose. "We can't get out!"

5

What *Is* This Stuff?

Cecil looked around the hall in a panic. Suddenly, a word above a door jumped out at him. "Custodian."

"There!" Cecil gasped. He pointed to Mr. O'Malley's door. "Quick! In there!"

Cecil and Carlos leaped for the doorknob. Would it be locked? Please, no, Cecil prayed.

Yes! It was open! They bolted inside, slamming the door behind them. Panting, they leaned up against the door. Cecil reached out. Click. He locked the door.

"Shhhh!" Cecil whispered. "You're breathing too loud. They might hear you!"

They held their ears against the door. Through the heavy metal door, they heard muffled footsteps coming closer. Cecil's stomach churned.

Voices shouted. Then the voices and footsteps stopped. Right in front of the custodian's door.

Cecil stared at the doorknob, eyes wide with fright. Next to him, Carlos stood against the door, tense with fear.

The doorknob jiggled. A stab of panic shot through Cecil. He *had* locked it, hadn't he?

The doorknob jiggled again, harder. Thoomp! A body banged up against the door.

Cecil almost fell backwards in fright. Carlos jumped away from the door. Color drained from his face.

"It's locked." Cecil heard a muffled voice just on the other side of the door. Reno's voice.

"Think they're in there?" That was Hendry.

"Doubt it," Reno said. "O'Malley always keeps it locked." There was a snicker. "He's afraid we'll steal his cleaning stuff." Laughter followed.

"Let's go. Maybe we'll see them at the bus stop." That was Reno again.

"Yeah. They're not gettin' away with *that!*" Hendry still sounded pretty mad. The voices and footsteps died away.

Cecil dropped down on the floor. He leaned his head back against a shelf of cleaning supplies.

"Whew!" he exclaimed. "I thought we were dust." He wiped his glasses and shut his eyes.

"Yeah, man," Carlos sighed. He flopped down across from Cecil. "You gotta put those nerdy brains of yours to work this weekend," he joked. "You gotta plan something."

"Uh-huh," Cecil said. He grinned. "You mean I don't have cottage cheese for brains?" Carlos grinned back.

Cecil sat up for a moment. He looked at the door. "I guess we'd better wait a while longer," he said. "I don't want to run into them at the bus stop."

"Me neither," Carlos agreed.

Cecil leaned back against the shelf again. A bottle toppled over. Clonk! It crashed onto the floor near Cecil. The cap flipped off. Some yellow liquid splashed on Cecil's arm. A scent of bananas filled the air.

"Sick!" Cecil said. He looked down at his arm.

POOF! Cecil froze. Where was his arm? In fact, where was *he?* He couldn't see himself—at all!

"Cecil? Cecil?" Carlos yelled. Cecil saw him looking right at him. "Where are you?"

"I—I'm right here! Right where I was before!" Cecil could hardly get the words out. His mouth was dry with fright. "You mean—you can't see me either?" he croaked.

"Jeez!" Carlos breathed. He trembled. "You're invisible!" He stared right where Cecil still sat.

Cecil reached out his hand. He touched his legs. He touched his arms. He could feel his body. But he couldn't see it. Cecil couldn't even see his clothes.

"Wha—what am I gonna do?" he wailed. "What is happening to me?" He could feel his hands trembling. But he couldn't see them.

He stared at the bright yellow bottle. He read the label aloud. "Clean 'Em Up—the world's most powerful cleanser. Cleans up the worst dirt. Effective for one hour." He blinked. He looked at Carlos. "What does that mean? Effective for one hour," he repeated.

"Does that mean you're invisible for only one hour?" Carlos asked, hopefully.

Cecil felt a little twinge of relief. "I hope that's what it means," he said. "World's most powerful cleanser. I'll say that again. It cleaned *me* right up," he joked halfheartedly.

"So in an hour, I can see you again?" Carlos asked. The color began returning to his face. "I sure hope so. I don't even know your mom. I sure don't wanna explain to her what happened to you," he said.

Cecil realized he felt a little dizzy. Probably fear. Could he be visible again? he wondered. Or would this be permanent?

Then Cecil blinked. "Wait a second," he said slowly to Carlos. "Wait a second." He began to grin. (Of course, Carlos couldn't tell.) "You know what?" Cecil jumped up. "This is fantastic! Cleans up the worst dirt!" He looked at Carlos. "Who are the worst dirt bags we know?" he asked.

"Hendry and Reno," Carlos said. He looked grumpy.

"So what. We don't want *them* invisible. I want to be able to see them coming!"

"No! That's not what I mean!" Cecil almost shouted. "If *we're* invisible, think what we can do! We can clean up those scum bags!"

Carlos looked puzzled. "I don't get it. What can we do?"

Cecil began to walk quickly around the small room. His heart pumped. Maybe this was the answer!

"Okay. If no one can see us, we can fix those jerks. We know enough stuff about them. We could really nail them!" Cecil began to laugh. "Oh, I can't wait!" he chuckled. "This is going to be awesome!"

He walked back over to the bottle where it lay on the floor. "I better cap this so we don't lose any more," he said. He reached out. He was careful not to get any more Clean 'Em Up on him. Then he'd probably be invisible even longer. He hoped that the directions about the hour part were right.

"Now I see," Carlos agreed. He began to smile. "Maybe this could be the beginning of the end of our troubles!"

Cecil screwed the Clean 'Em Up cap on carefully. Then he frowned. (Not that Carlos could tell.)

"I hope one-hour effectiveness means it wears off in an hour." Cecil glanced down at his watch. There was nothing there but thin air. Of course. He kept forgetting.

Carlos jumped up. He looked in the direction of

Cecil's voice. "So, let's make some plans," he said. Carlos couldn't wait to get started.

"First, think about what the label means," Cecil said. He shoved his invisible hands in his invisible pockets. "If the directions are right, we'll have an hour to do something to each guy."

Cecil picked up the bottle. Carlos flinched. The bottle appeared to be floating by itself. Cecil shook the bottle.

"Hmmmm," he said. He put it back on the shelf. "I'm sure there's enough left for two times. Okay. First, what bothers Hendry?" he asked Carlos. He paced up and down in the tiny room.

"Uh—Mrs. Harvey?" Carlos asked.

Cecil grinned. Carlos was moving his head back and forth trying to follow the sound of Cecil's voice. He looked as if he were watching a tennis game.

"Nah. Mrs. Harvey doesn't bother Hendry. It's Song! He's afraid of Song!" Cecil exclaimed. "So, all we have to do is get him to do something that ticks Song off!"

"Hey! Yeah!" Carlos said. "Song already thinks Hendry is a loser." A grin stretched across his face. "Remember what he said at lunch? The first day of school?"

"Uh-huh," Cecil agreed. "Plus, think of what Song says in math class or homeroom when Hendry does something stupid. Song wouldn't have any problem hassling Hendry—if he had a good reason," Cecil said. He stopped next to a sponge mop. He twirled the mop handle between his hands.

"Hey, stop it, man! You're givin' me the creeps!" Carlos said. He shuddered. "All I can see is the mop wiggling around!"

Cecil laughed. He let go of the sponge mop. "So, if we're invisible, we'll do something to Song. And we'll make Song think Hendry did it. Then we can just watch while Hendry gets his face beat into the ground. This is gonna be good!"

"Great!" Carlos said, grinning. "How about Reno?" He kept moving his head to follow the sound of Cecil's voice.

Cecil stopped next to a cart loaded with cleaning supplies. "Yeah, Reno," he said slowly.

"So what's the plan?" Carlos asked. He looked over at the cart. Cecil was rolling it back and forth. "Hey, cut it out. That looks too weird. The cart rolling by itself, I mean."

"Sorry," Cecil said, smiling an invisible smile. "Okay—Reno," he said. "He really gets to me. This has to be good," Cecil said.

"Yeah, I agree," Carlos said.

"You know what it is?" Cecil asked. "I've been thinking about it. He's sneaky. He's a liar. He thinks of the worst things to do. Then he hides behind Hendry. He's a phony with all the teachers and stuff. 'Sorry, Mrs. Harvey.' " Cecil mimicked Reno's voice.

"I'm gonna need more time for Reno," Cecil continued. "I'll just keep my eye on him. I know I'll think of something. We'll find a way!"

"I think you did it," Carlos said. He got to his feet. "Clean 'Em Up is the answer. I'd like to shake your hand, man." He stopped. "If I could see it!"

"Yeah," Cecil said slowly. He looked at the bottle sitting on the shelf. "Hopefully, before too long, we can shake on it."

6

Hendry Gets His

Carlos looked at his watch. "It's gotta be almost time, man," he said. "I don't know exactly when you became invisible. But it had to be shortly after the last bell. And that was a little over an hour ago."

Cecil felt nervous. He wished he could see his watch.

Carlos stared at where Cecil should be standing. Cecil looked at where his outstretched hands should be. Nothing! They were still invisible. Panic gripped him.

"What now?" he almost shouted. He stared at Carlos. "What am I gonna do?" He felt lightheaded. "It's been over an hour. I just know it has."

"Carlos! Help me!" he begged. "Should we call the fire department? An ambulance? What can we do? No one will believe us!"

"Just relax," Carlos assured him. Carlos was pretty scared too, but he didn't want Cecil to know. "Just give it a few more minutes. You'll be visible any minute now. I just know it," he said more confidently than he felt.

POOF! Cecil blinked. His arms and legs appeared! He stared for a moment at his hands. He felt all over them. He was visible again!

"Yes! Yes!" Cecil yelled. A wave of relief washed over him. "I'm back! Yeah!"

Then he stared at Carlos. Carlos wiped the sweat from his forehead. "Oh, man," he breathed. "That was too close."

"Whew," Cecil said. "Looks like I wasn't the only nervous one!" He wiped his forehead with his sleeve. He took his glasses off. He wiped them with his shirt.

"Well, let's get out of here," Cecil said. "We'll do a game plan this weekend. Come Monday, look out Hendry and Reno!"

Cecil walked over to the bottle of Clean 'Em Up. "Do you think Mr. O'Malley will notice it's gone?" he asked Carlos. "I kinda hate to take it."

"Nah. Don't worry about it," Carlos said. "We'll only use a little bit. Then we'll put it back." Carlos gestured at all the cleaning supplies. "Look at all the stuff he's got in here. He'll never miss it."

Cecil shook the bottle. "There's not much left in here," he said. "Oh well. We gotta do it. It's for a good cause," he said.

He unzipped his backpack. Then he dropped the bottle inside.

"Mr. O'Malley would probably think it was a great idea. He doesn't like those jerks either," Cecil reminded Carlos.

Cecil walked to the door. He unlocked it and peered around the doorjamb. The halls were empty and silent.

Together, the two boys walked out, closing the door behind them. Once outside the school, they looked up and down for Hendry and Reno. No one was around. They walked to the bus stop.

"Do you think Mr. O'Malley knows what this stuff does?" Cecil asked.

The bus heaved up, huffing its brakes. The doors wheezed open. The boys climbed in.

"I dunno," Carlos said. "I don't think so. Wouldn't he have told us about it? You know, when he helped us in the hall?" He dropped down into a seat. Cecil dropped down next to him.

"Yeah. You're probably right," he agreed. Then he sat up straight. He grinned. "All I know is, I can't wait until Monday!"

****

The weekend passed quickly. Cecil and Carlos spent hours on the phone making plans. They both agreed. Hendry would be the easiest. "That's cause he's so stupid!" Carlos commented Sunday night on the phone. They laughed.

"Definitely, the toughest one is gonna be Reno," Cecil said. "We'll just have to keep our eyes open. We'll get that weasel! And I can't wait."

"Me either. See ya before school," Carlos said.

"You bet," Cecil said. "Bye." He hung up the phone. Tomorrow couldn't come too soon to suit him.

****

Monday morning came. Cecil checked his backpack twice. He wanted to be sure his Clean 'Em Up was safe inside.

Despite their plans, Cecil dreaded seeing Reno and Hendry. He felt better in homeroom, though. Song sat with them. So all the bullies could do was glare at him and Carlos.

Just wait until lunch. That was when they planned to get Hendry. They had an hour for lunch, so they had to time it just right.

When the lunch bell rang, Cecil rushed to his locker. He took out the bottle of Clean 'Em Up. Then he shoved his backpack back inside.

Cecil walked casually into the boys' bathroom. Carlos was already there. Thankfully, no one else was around.

"This is it!" Carlos said. His eyes gleamed with excitement.

Cecil's hands shook a little. He unscrewed the cap. "I—I hope it works the right way," he said slowly. "If—if we're invisible too long, we're gonna get into trouble!"

"Ah, don't sweat it," Carlos said. He held out his hand for some Clean 'Em Up. "Are you going first?" he asked.

Cecil noticed that Carlos' hand shook a little. He pulled it back. "Does it hurt?" he asked.

Cecil grinned. He couldn't believe Carlos was actually scared. Tough Carlos, who was ready to take on Hendry!

"Nah," Cecil said, grinning. Cecil poured a little out in his own hand. The scent of bananas filled the room again.

POOF! Cecil vanished.

"Whoa!" Cecil laughed out loud. "This is wild, man!" He began jumping around. Carlos watched the bottle dance away from him all by itself.

"Hey, pal! Hurry up!" Carlos said urgently. "We've only got an hour, right? Aren't you the one who's worried about getting back to class on time?"

"Yeah, you're right," Cecil said. He walked over to Carlos. "Hold out your hand," he said. He poured a thin stream of yellow liquid onto Carlos' hand.

POOF! Carlos disappeared into thin air.

"Yeah!" they shouted together. Cecil set the bottle down behind the trash can. "It should be safe here," he said. He looked where he thought Carlos was.

"Let's go," Cecil said. "We don't have much time."

7

Hendry Learns His Manners

The boys raced out of the boys' bathroom. They headed for the quad. Students sat in the sunshine eating their lunches. Some stereos blared.

"Where is Hendry the jerk?" Cecil whispered to Carlos. He scanned the students. "There!" he said in a low voice. "Under that tree. See? Right next to Reno, that little weasel."

"Now, where's Song?" Carlos asked. He looked around. "Hah! There! Good—he's sitting pretty close to them."

"Okay. Let's go," Cecil whispered. Together, they walked over to Hendry.

"Oh, man, this is so funny!" Cecil said softly to Carlos. They walked by dozens of students. Everyone stared right through them. Carlos even put his face right in front of a girl's nose. She just kept eating her sandwich.

"Shhhh," Cecil whispered. They crept up on Hendry. Cecil grabbed Hendry's lunch bag. Carlos grabbed Hendry's soda.

"Hey!" Hendry yelled. Cecil could see he was scared. Hendry jumped up. He turned around and stared into thin air.

Quickly, Cecil threw Hendry's lunch right next to Song. It clonked the back of Song's head. At the same time, Carlos put his thumb over the soda can. He shook it hard. Then he sprayed the soda on Hendry's head. It sprayed all over everyone sitting close by too.

"Hey!" Song roared. He jumped to his feet. He rubbed his head. He looked down at the ground. Then he picked up Hendry's lunch bag. It read "Hendry" across the front in big letters.

Song turned around. His eyes narrowed. A few drops of soda dripped down his forehead. Hendry was standing about five feet away. He looked confused and scared. Soda ran down his face.

All around them, students had stopped eating lunch.

No one was talking. A little laughter rippled through the air. Some kids whispered. And everyone was watching. Cecil and Carlos both choked back laughter.

"What do you think you're doin'?" Song yelled. "You got somethin' wrong with you? Do you need a lesson?" he roared.

Hendry began backing up. He stepped on a girl's lunch.

"Hey!" she complained. She pushed at Hendry's leg. Hendry's eyes were fixed on Song. Song was walking menacingly toward him.

"You idiot!" he barked. He wiped some soda off his forehead. "Wanna fight? 'Cause *I* do!" He held up his fists. He glared at Hendry.

Hendry backed up a few more steps. No more Mr. Tough Guy now. Even from where he stood, Cecil could see Hendry shaking. What a wimp, he thought. Big talker, but when it came to facing someone more his own size, Hendry chickened out.

"N—no," Hendry whimpered. "It—it was an accident. I swear it!" he almost whispered. "I—I didn't do it!"

Cecil could see the other students giving each other looks. Some even smirked and whispered. Cecil knew what they were probably thinking. It was clear that nobody cared much for Hendry.

"You didn't do it, huh? Well, I'm gonna make sure we don't have any more 'accidents,' " Song said. He flexed his fingers. He walked up even closer to Hendry and shoved his face into Hendry's face.

Then Song gave Hendry a push. Hendry flew backwards. He landed on his behind. "Ow!" he said. Laughter filled the air. Cecil and Carlos joined in.

On the ground, Hendry curled up in a little ball. "Please!" he said. "Please don't hit me! It was an accident!"

Song looked at Hendry squirming on the ground. "I don't know how a lunch can fly five feet through the air," he said in disgust. "Or soda spray out of your can. But you're not worth fighting. You wimp," he sneered.

"I'm tired of you and your bullying," Song continued. "I don't need much of an excuse to take care of you once and for all. So, you quit hassling people around here," he warned. "Or I'm gonna rearrange your face. And that's a promise. I don't care *who* you're hassling," he threatened. "Got it?" Song leaned down and pulled Hendry's T-shirt neck up. He stared at him, nose to nose.

"Y—yes," Hendry stammered. "Okay. No more hassling. Promise."

"Hey! Where are you, man? I want to high five you!" Cecil whispered.

"Here!" Carlos said, reaching out an arm.

They high-fived each other. "Yes!" Cecil said. "Gotcha, Hendry! That worked better than we even thought! Song was awesome! Now maybe Hendry will even leave us alone! One down, one to go!"

Cecil and Carlos raced for the boys' bathroom. They planned to reappear inside stalls.

On their way through the quad, Cecil noticed a blue

custodian's uniform. It looked like Mr. O'Malley had seen it all. And he was smiling.

They jogged around a corner. A horrible thought burst into Cecil's brain. What if the second time he used Clean 'Em Up, it was stronger?

What if it took him longer to come back this time?

What if he couldn't come back at all?

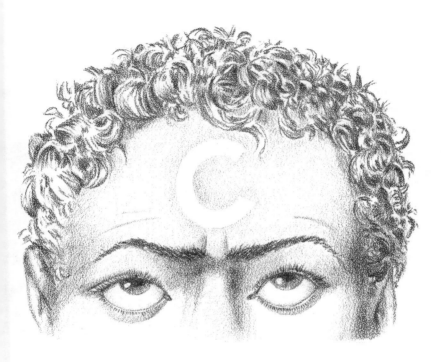

8

The Yellow C

Hearts thumping, Cecil and Carlos rushed into the boys' bathroom. No one was inside.

"Now we wait," Cecil said. He hoisted himself up on the counter. He looked in the mirror. The empty bathroom reflected back at him. No one was in the mirror he was staring at. It was weird.

"Since I've already vanished once, do—do you think it's gonna be harder for me to come back again?" he asked. He hoped Carlos would say something to make him feel better.

"Who knows?" Carlos' voice said at his elbow.

"Hey!" Cecil said. "We almost forgot! Is the bottle still behind the trash can?"

Cecil slipped off the counter. He walked quickly toward the trash can. What if Mr. O'Malley had come in to clean? What if he had taken it? Then they wouldn't be able to take care of Reno.

"It's here!" Cecil said. He grabbed the bottle off the floor.

Carlos ran some water in the sink to wash the sticky soda off his hands. It was funny to see the soap bubble up over nothing. He dried his hands on a paper towel. The paper towel jumped around in the air by itself.

Just then, the bell rang to end lunch.

"It's time!" Cecil said. "An hour is almost up! Quick! Get into a stall," he said.

Cecil saw a door open and close. Carlos began laughing. "Sure hope no one tries to get in here with me," he joked.

"Shhh," Cecil warned. He hid in the next stall. He locked it. Then he waited. Cecil shut his eyes. He didn't dare look.

POOF! Cecil's eyes flew open. He was back! He looked down. He saw his Nikes and his jeans. He was visible again!

POOF! "Yeah!" Carlos yelled from the next stall. "All right!"

"We made it!" Cecil cried.

They both burst out of their stalls and through the bathroom door. There, standing outside the bathroom with her arms folded was Mrs. Harvey.

"All right, what's going on in there?" Mrs. Harvey demanded. She frowned. "What's all the 'yeah' and 'all right' stuff? Smoking? Or worse?"

"N—nothing," Cecil stammered. He thought quickly. "We— ah—Carlos just told me a funny joke, that's all," he fibbed.

"Really?" Mrs. Harvey said. Icicles dripped from her words. "Well, then, you won't mind turning out your pockets." She planted her feet in front of them.

Cecil set the bottle down quickly. Mrs. Harvey glanced at it. Then she looked back at Cecil.

"What's that?" Mrs. Harvey asked.

"Ah—ah—I found it in there. I'll take it to Mr. O'Malley. His office is right by my locker," Cecil said quickly.

"Hmph. All right, pockets. Now!" Mrs. Harvey commanded.

Cecil turned his pockets inside out. His hands trembled a little. Some change. His bus pass. The key to his house. Lint.

Carlos did the same. The two boys looked at Mrs.

Harvey.

"Okay," Mrs. Harvey sighed. "Don't get yourselves into trouble. It's too easy to do," she said. She turned and left.

"Whew," Cecil said. He wiped his glasses. "That was a little too close." He frowned. "We'd better get to class. See you in math. Then, we'll have to just watch and see how we can get to Reno."

Cecil daydreamed through history again. Boring, boring. Math was next. Math—and Hendry and Reno. His stomach churned a little at the thought. He wondered if Song's threat would be enough for Hendry. Would Hendry stop bugging him and Carlos? They'd soon find out.

Cecil stopped in front of the door to math class. He took a deep breath and turned the knob. Hendry was heading toward his seat. Cecil stared at his back.

"Hey, man," Song said to Carlos and Cecil from across the room. Cecil looked over. Song held up a hand. He smiled. Cecil smiled back.

Cecil saw Hendry flinch at the sound of Song's voice. "Hey, Song," Cecil said as he slid into his desk. Song was definitely all right.

"Hey, man!" Reno exclaimed to Hendry. "What's on your face? On your forehead?" He started laughing rudely at Hendry. "What does it stand for? Cool? Cute? Cat food?"

Hendry looked worried. He reached his hand up to rub his forehead. Cecil stared. A big yellow letter *C* shone in the middle of Hendry's forehead.

Cecil and Carlos turned and stared at each other. Their eyes opened wide.

"No way!" Cecil breathed. It must stand for "Clean 'Em Up"! He grinned at Carlos. "We branded him!"

"What is it?" Hendry asked. He looked down at his hand. There was nothing there.

"It's still there, man!" Reno cackled. By this time, everyone in the class was looking at Hendry. Kids were starting to laugh.

Hendry's face turned bright red. He scrubbed at his forehead.

Well, why not, Cecil thought. He took a deep breath, stood up, and walked over to Hendry.

"So. Does it smell like bananas?" he asked Hendry.

Hendry sniffed at his hand. He looked shocked. "Yeah!" he said.

Cecil snorted. "Figures," he said. "Good luck," he added. He stared hard at Hendry.

Hendry's jaw dropped. "How—how—do you—?" he began. He looked scared. Then he looked down quickly. Cecil strode back to his desk, hiding a smile.

Good. Maybe Song's warning would work—on Hendry, anyway. And the yellow *C*—Hendry probably figured Cecil had something to do with it. And he was bothered too. A lot.

One down and one to go. He and Carlos still had to settle with Reno.

Reno stared over at Cecil and curled his lip into a

sneer. You just wait, Cecil thought. I'll wipe that smile off your face!

The math teacher droned on. Cecil kept watching the clock. He looked over at Carlos. He kept looking at the clock too. Once, their eyes met, and they grinned. He wouldn't look at Reno though.

The bell finally rang. Carlos and Cecil walked out the door with Song. Cecil looked back over his shoulder to see Hendry still scrubbing at his forehead with his fist. His forehead was bright red from all the rubbing. Reno was standing next to him, frowning.

After homeroom, Carlos and Cecil made a quick stop at their lockers. They passed Song as they headed out of the building. "See you, Song," Cecil said as they walked out. Song raised a hand and grinned.

"Could you believe that mark?" Cecil exclaimed to Carlos. He grinned broadly. "That was great!"

"Uh-huh," said Carlos. He grinned back. "Hendry's worried now! Did you see how he looked at you when you asked him about the banana smell? He looked scared!"

"Yup!" Cecil said. "And now, on to Reno!"

Laughing, Cecil and Carlos dashed to the bus stop. From the corner of his eye, Cecil thought he saw a blue custodian's uniform disappear around the corner of the school. Mr. O'Malley was sure busy.

Cars whizzed by. Finally, the bus lurched to the curb. The doors hissed. Cecil and Carlos climbed in and dropped down into some seats.

"That was so much fun," Carlos said, grinning. He almost bounced up and down in his seat with excitement. "What a scene. Hendry flat on his behind." He slapped his own knee in glee. "Did you see the look on that meathead's face?"

Cecil and Carlos grinned at each other.

Now that they had taken care of Hendry, Cecil really wanted to get Reno. He stared out the window of the bus thinking about what they could do. Suddenly, it came to him. Why hadn't he thought of it sooner?

"That's it!" Cecil exclaimed.

"What's it?" asked Carlos. "What are you talking about?"

"It's just perfect. I can't believe I didn't think of this earlier," added Cecil.

"What's perfect?" Carlos asked again, getting impatient.

"You know those office call slips that Reno was bragging about the other day?" Cecil asked. "The ones with Mrs. Harvey's forged signatures? All we have to do is make sure that Mrs. Harvey sees those slips. Once she sees that whole stack of blank slips, she'll flip.

"And Reno's such a phony," Cecil continued. "He's always brown-nosing. Once Mrs. Harvey learns of his little scam, she'll never trust him again!" He only hoped it would go as well as it had with Hendry.

"You are a genius!" Carlos exclaimed. "Reno will be history. I can't wait!"

9

The Plan for Reno

The next morning, Cecil and Carlos met at their lockers. The boys walked together to homeroom. They sat down next to Song.

Cecil looked across the room. Hendry was shooting off his big mouth to Reno. Cecil elbowed Carlos. The yellow *C* still glimmered on Hendry's forehead. His forehead looked raw from scrubbing. Cecil smiled. Hendry must have been up all night trying to scrub it off.

Hendry looked over at Cecil. Cecil narrowed his eyes at Hendry and smirked. Hendry looked away.

Hah! Cecil thought. It felt good to stare Hendry down. He hid a smile. Reno just looked confused.

Cecil elbowed Carlos and pointed to Hendry. "Gotcha!" he whispered. Carlos grinned.

Song leaned over. "Did you guys have something to do with that *C* on his forehead?" Song whispered, grinning. "How did you do it?"

"Nah, not really," Cecil said quickly. He couldn't let Song find out about the Clean 'Em Up. It had to stay a secret. "It looks funny, doesn't it? I bet it stands for confused!"

"Yeah, or cheesehead," Carlos said, grinning.

"How about cabbagebrain?" Song added. The three boys started to laugh.

"Now, class," Miss Reed said weakly. "Now, class. Please settle down."

Finally, the class fell silent. Someone read the bulletin. The bell rang. Everyone left.

"See you at lunch," Cecil said to Carlos and Song. He hurried out the door to the gym. Thinking about their Clean 'Em Up plan for Reno made him smile.

Later, Cecil lined up with everyone in the gym. He had his uniform on. It made him look even more like the "before" of a weight-lifting ad. He sighed. Would he ever bulk up? Maybe he should try working out. That would help.

At the front of the gym, he heard the familiar whine of Reno's voice. He always sounded as if he was talking through his nose. Cecil frowned. What a loser!

Wait! What was *Reno* doing in his P.E. class? Reno was standing next to his P.E. teacher. The teacher was signing something. With a growing feeling of dread, Cecil listened.

"Just take this transfer slip back to the office," the teacher said. "Then you can join the class."

Oh no, Cecil groaned to himself. And Song wasn't in this class to help him out either. Or Carlos. Why did this have to happen to him? He sighed.

Reno returned in his P.E. uniform. The class was warming up. Reno strutted over to Cecil. He looked over at the P.E. teacher. The teacher wasn't looking.

"Gonna work on those tiny muscles, skinny?" Reno smirked. He began stretching.

Cecil tightened his mouth. He hated sneaky guys like Reno. And he wouldn't lower himself to say anything back to him either. If he did, Reno would just get worse anyway.

"Whatsa matter?" Reno taunted. "Ain't got yer huge buddy Carlos to help ya?" He grinned evilly.

"Shut up, you jerk," Cecil said through tight lips. He could take stuff about himself. But no one was going to say stuff about his friend.

"Oooh, getting tough, are we?" Reno sneered. "How about later we see how tough you are?"

Cecil looked away. But he cringed inside. What did Reno mean by *later?*

After showering, Cecil hurried to study hall. He had homework to do. And maybe he'd get some peace too.

Cecil sat down by the window. Then he looked at the front of the room. His jaw dropped when he saw who was there.

Mrs. Harvey was in charge of his study hall. That wasn't a surprise. But next to Mrs. Harvey stood Reno. He was holding a piece of paper again. He was smiling his phony grin at Mrs. Harvey.

"Fine," Mrs. Harvey was saying to Reno. She smiled. "I run a tight ship, you know. You do your work, and we'll get along just fine." She scribbled her signature on the piece of paper.

Oh no! Cecil felt as if someone had just punched him in the stomach. Why was Reno following him around? Cecil almost groaned aloud. Three classes! Now he had Reno in three whole classes!

"Of course, Mrs. Harvey," Reno said smoothly. His eyes opened wide. "I really like to use my study halls wisely."

Cecil bent his head low over his work. Maybe Reno wouldn't see him in here. What had Reno meant by that "We'll see how tough you are later" thing he'd said in P.E.? Were he and Carlos going to get dusted?

Cecil waited nervously all during study hall. He watched Reno from the corner of his eye. But Reno didn't do anything. Except flatter Mrs. Harvey. What a jerk!

That afternoon, Cecil opened the door to math class. He took a deep breath. Hendry looked up. Cecil just stared right back. The yellow *C* still gleamed from the middle of Hendry's forehead. Hendry lowered his eyes at Cecil's stare.

Then Cecil looked over at Reno. Reno was busy whispering to someone. He must have felt Cecil's eyes on him. He turned and narrowed his eyes at Cecil. In spite of himself, Cecil felt his stomach churn a little.

Did Reno have something terrible planned for him and Carlos? Or just for him—in P.E. class? He felt a little sick. Study hall was probably pretty safe. Mrs. Harvey would see to that. But there were too many bad things that could happen in P.E. class.

"Take out your homework," the math teacher directed. Papers shuffled and books slapped open on desks. Cecil took out his homework. From the corner of his eye, he saw Reno whispering to Hendry.

They weren't taking papers out. They weren't even looking for homework. They probably hadn't even done it. Pretty stupid—especially for the first couple weeks of school.

Cecil wondered what those two had planned. How were they going to get out of not having their homework?

The next minute, Cecil got his answer. The classroom door opened. A runner from the office came in. He held a bunch of call slips.

The teacher stopped talking. She took the call slips. "Reno Wilkins and Hendry Lawson." She frowned. "You're to report to the library. That's strange. Hmph." She shrugged her shoulders.

So that was their plan. Get called out of class with Reno's fake call slips. Those jerks. He looked over at Carlos. Carlos nodded his head. He saw it too.

The two boys were already out of their seats. They were trying to hide their smiles as they took the slips.

"Come back as soon as you're done," she sighed. She turned her attention to the rest of the class.

Cecil stared at Reno's backpack. Reno had left it under his desk. Where did Reno keep those call slips? Were they in one of the pockets?

He had to find out. It was part of the plan. And the plan was looking better all the time. Especially now that Reno was in his study hall. And—he almost laughed out loud—Mrs. Harvey was their study hall supervisor.

Students exchanged homework. The buzz in the room got louder as everyone checked answers. Cecil looked around quickly. Then he reached out his toe and hooked Reno's backpack strap. He pulled the backpack under his own desk.

Cecil looked around again. He reached down. Quickly, he opened two pockets. His fingers shook a little. No call slips there.

He glanced up. The teacher was busy helping a student. He undid another pocket. There! A feeling of power surged through him. He started to grin.

A thick bundle of call slips fattened the pocket. He flipped through them quickly. At the bottom of each one was written *D. Harvey, V.P.* Yes! Now he was ready for Plan B. He'd wipe that fake smile off Reno's face and love every minute.

****

Cecil had trouble sleeping that night. He tossed and turned under his covers. He couldn't stop thinking about their plan for Reno.

****

As soon as Cecil got to school, he hurried to the office. He checked the nurse's schedule. So far, so good. She was at Graves Junior High today. His plan would work today!

He met Carlos at the lockers. Cecil told him the plan.

"No way!" Carlos said, grinning. "Do you want any help?" he asked eagerly.

"No. Thanks," Cecil said. "I think it would look bad. Two of us shouldn't get out of class at the same time. It would be too risky." He shut his locker. Together, they went to homeroom.

There sat Hendry. The *C* was as bright as ever. A constant reminder. Cecil smirked. Too bad for Hendry. Kids were laughing at him all the time.

Cecil watched Reno during homeroom. Reno

whispered to Hendry the whole time. Uh-oh, Cecil thought. Was he planning something?

Cecil watched the clock in his first class. P.E. was next. He flinched. Had Reno already plotted something to do to him?

But P.E. class passed by. Reno had been on another team. After class, Reno had just said one thing. They were standing in line for towels. "Outta my way, skinny," Reno muttered to him. He shoved past Cecil.

Cecil had tightened his mouth. He kept quiet. He could wait for his revenge.

Study hall was next. Cecil felt his muscles tense. At his locker, he slipped the Clean 'Em Up into his backpack.

What if Reno didn't have his backpack with him? What if he had taken out the phony call slips? Or what if Reno wasn't even in study hall today?

Cecil walked into study hall. Reno was there. And his backpack sat under his desk. Just as Cecil sat down, Reno looked over.

"Huh!" he snorted. "What are *you* gonna do in study hall?" he sneered. "You probably don't have any work at all. You nerds always do your homework a month ahead. Right?" He laughed at his own joke.

Other students turned and looked at Cecil. He felt his face burn. You wait, Reno, he muttered silently. You just wait.

Mrs. Harvey called the roll. Reno sat up straight. He smiled at Mrs. Harvey.

"Here, ma'am!" Reno said loudly. Mrs. Harvey's stern face relaxed a little. "Hello, Reno," she said.

What a sneak, Cecil thought. He couldn't wait. Mrs. Harvey wouldn't be smiling at Reno much longer.

"Get to work," Mrs. Harvey ordered. Then she sat down at the teacher's desk and began looking through a stack of papers.

Cecil crossed his fingers for luck. He took a deep breath. Calm down, he told himself. He arranged his face in a mask of discomfort. Then he walked up to Mrs. Harvey.

"Yes?" Mrs. Harvey looked annoyed at being interrupted. "What is it?" she sighed.

"Uh, Mrs. Harvey? I don't feel so good," Cecil fibbed. "It's my stomach. And my little sister was throwing up all night," he added.

Mrs. Harvey looked worried. She leaned away from him.

"All right," she said. She scribbled on a hall pass. "Go to the office. They'll put you in the sickroom. If you don't feel better, you might have to go home," she said.

Hah! Cecil chuckled to himself. Throwing up was always the best excuse. Nobody wanted you around then. Headaches never got you anywhere.

He grabbed his backpack and headed for the office. Everything went according to plan. He sneaked out of the sickroom. Once in the boys' bathroom, he took out the bottle of Clean 'Em Up. He looked at his watch. He was nervous. But getting back at Reno was worth the risk.

10
Gotcha!

Cecil held the bottle of yellow liquid in his shaking hands. He removed the cap, turned the bottle over, and the yellow liquid dripped onto his hand. Once again, the smell of bananas overpowered him.

POOF! He was gone! His heart raced. He slipped the bottle of Clean 'Em Up inside his backpack, which he set behind the trashcan.

THE GOTCHA PLOT

Cecil hurried down the halls. He looked in the window of the study hall door. Reno was staring out the open window. An open book lay on his desk. Reno probably hadn't even looked at it once. Reno's backpack was still on the floor.

Some students studied. He could see some were writing notes. A few were whispering. They got dirty looks from Mrs. Harvey.

He'd just open the door and slip in. Maybe they'd think it was the wind.

He pulled the door open and squeezed in. He let the door swing shut.

Mrs. Harvey looked up. She looked puzzled. Then she looked over at the windows. Mrs. Harvey sighed and turned back to her papers.

Cecil walked over to Reno's desk. He bent down and reached for the backpack. He felt the pocket. Yes! The call slips were still there!

Now for the best part of his plan. Mrs. Harvey patrolled the aisles every now and then. She'd get up and walk around the room to check on the students.

All Cecil had to do was wait for Mrs. Harvey to patrol again. He hoped it wouldn't be too long. He crouched next to Reno's desk and watched the clock. When was Mrs. Harvey going to get up again?

Time passed slowly as Cecil waited. Finally, Mrs. Harvey sighed. She got up and began walking up and down the aisles.

Cecil waited. Before too long, Mrs. Harvey was in Reno's aisle. Now! She was two desks away from Reno. Cecil opened the backpack pocket quickly. He picked up the backpack.

Reno's face froze in horror. He watched the backpack lift by itself into the air. Swiftly, Cecil shook it in the aisle. Dozens of call slips fluttered to the ground. Then he dumped the backpack on Reno's desk. A few more call slips slid out of the pocket onto Reno's desk.

"Ah-ah-achoo!" Cecil faked a loud sneeze. He wanted to be sure Mrs. Harvey would see all the call slips on the floor.

Mrs. Harvey stopped. She smiled at Reno. "Got kind of a mess here, don't we?" she joked. Then she bent down and began picking up the call slips.

"Uh—no! Mrs. Harvey! I'll—I'll do that!" Reno shouted. He scrambled to the floor. He almost knocked over Mrs. Harvey. "Please! It's my mess!"

Reno began scrabbling around, stuffing call slips into his hands. Cecil stood by, his shoulders shaking with invisible laughter. Too much! he thought. But the best was still coming.

Before too long, Mrs. Harvey glanced down at a call slip. "What's this?" she exclaimed. Then her face darkened. She whipped around and glared at Reno, who was still grabbing call slips off the floor.

"What is the meaning of this?" she trumpeted. She snatched more call slips from Reno's hand. "Blank call slips?" she thundered. "With *my* signature on every one? I never signed these!"

The color drained from Reno's face. "Come with me, young man. You have a lot of explaining to do!"

Gotcha! Cecil wanted to yell.

Mrs. Harvey almost yanked Reno from the room. She slammed the door. Behind them, the room exploded in laughter and loud talking.

"What a loser!"

"He finally got his!"

"Reno is toast!"

Cecil could hardly keep from laughing out loud with them. He couldn't believe it! It had worked! Wait until he told Carlos. He looked up at the clock. Time to get going. But first he wanted to hear what Mrs. Harvey was telling Reno.

He slipped out of the back door. No one even noticed. He walked up behind Mrs. Harvey and Reno. Down the hall, he saw Mr. O'Malley pushing a sponge mop.

Reno was backed up against the lockers. Cecil blinked twice. Right in the middle of Reno's forehead was a shiny, yellow *C!* All right! Cecil grinned. Now there'd be no doubt about who had taken care of Reno.

Mrs. Harvey was right in Reno's face, yelling. "I could have you expelled for this!" Mrs. Harvey fumed. "Your parents are going to get called on this one. This is going in your permanent file. And all your teachers will be notified.

" 'Sorry, ma'am,'—that's your line, isn't it?" Mrs. Harvey continued. "Well, don't think about trying it again."

Reno shrank back. Cecil grinned. If Reno could have clawed his way through the lockers to hide, he would have.

"And of course you'll be suspended," Mrs. Harvey barked.

A smirk flitted across Reno's face. Mrs. Harvey should know better than that, thought Cecil. Reno will love suspension.

Mrs. Harvey laughed curtly. "It's going to be *in-school* suspension. You'll come every day and sit all day in my office. You'll be lucky if any teacher ever trusts you again."

Reno's face fell. He looked as if he were blinking back tears. Serves you right, Cecil snapped silently.

"And wipe that letter *C* off your forehead," Mrs. Harvey barked. "What does it stand for? Cretin?"

The bell rang. Uh-oh, Cecil thought. He raced for the boys' bathroom. His hour was running out. But it was an hour well spent.

He rounded the corner and headed into the restroom. He grabbed his backpack and jumped into a stall. Nervously, he waited.

POOF! He was back! Cecil hurried to the office and slipped into the sickroom. Then he walked out slowly. He got his time stamp with no problem. Study hall was over, so Cecil headed to his next class. He couldn't wait to tell Carlos at lunch!

Cecil headed to his locker before lunch. As he rounded the corner, he ran smack into someone.

"Sorry!" a voice said. Cecil looked around. It was Reno. His face was blotchy, except for the letter *C* in the center of his forehead.

"That's okay," Cecil answered. He stared at Reno.

"Did—do you know anything about this?" Reno asked, pointing to his forehead. "It won't come off. It smells just like bananas. Just like Hendry's."

"Sorreeee," Cecil said sarcastically. "I really couldn't say. See ya." Cecil strode away.

Carlos waited at the lockers.

"Carlos, you're not going to believe it," Cecil crowed to Carlos. Carlos' eyes grew round as he listened to the story of Reno and Mrs. Harvey.

"Awesome, man!" Carlos exclaimed. He slapped Cecil on the back. "You did it!"

Then Cecil unzipped his backpack. He took out the bottle of Clean 'Em Up. "I think we can put this back in Mr. O'Malley's closet for now," Cecil said. "We know where it is if we ever need to do more cleaning up."

The bottle felt unusually light. So Cecil took off the cap. It was empty. It was totally empty! He hadn't realized. He had used it all up.

"Hey, Carlos," Cecil croaked. "The Clean 'Em Up is gone! I used it up! What if we need it again?"

"We'll just get another bottle from Mr. O'Malley's closet," Carlos replied.

"But this was the only bottle," Cecil added. "I wonder if he'll order more. Should we ask him?"

Carlos slumped against the lockers. "How can we do that? He'll know we took it."

Cecil sighed. "It's been great stuff. I'd feel a lot better if we had a supply around. Just in case." He slammed his locker shut.

Carlos and Cecil headed down the hall. Mr. O'Malley was polishing a classroom door knob.

"Hello, boys," he said. His eyes twinkled. "Got everything under control these days?" he asked.

"Sure do," Cecil answered. He exchanged glances with Carlos.

"Good," Mr. O'Malley said. He straightened up. "Well," he said, "gotta go do some paperwork. It's time to check in my new cleaning supplies." He grinned at Cecil and Carlos. "I hate paperwork. Cleaning up is more fun."

Check in supplies? Had he ordered more Clean 'Em Up? A little flash of hope ran through Cecil.

"Uh, yeah," Cecil said. "We hate paperwork too. Ours is called homework," he joked. "See you," he said. Together, he and Carlos walked outside.

After lunch, the boys returned to their lockers. When Cecil opened his, a bottle fell out. It almost clonked him on the head. A small piece of paper fluttered down after it.

"Hey!" he exclaimed. "What's this?" Cecil reached down and picked up the bottle. It was Clean 'Em Up.

"Hey!" Carlos said. He held up a bottle. "I got one too!"

Cecil picked up the note. "Listen to this!" he said. He began reading:

"Here's another bottle. Just in case you need to do a little cleaning up. But I don't think you'll really need it. Gotcha!

A Friend."

"Yeah!" Cecil shouted. He grinned at Carlos. A Friend. That had to be Mr. O'Malley!

Cecil looked at Carlos. "You know, I think he's right," he said slowly. "I don't think we will need it. We can handle those jerks. Reno and Hendry won't even look at us any more. They know we aren't afraid of them now." He smiled at Carlos. "In fact, I think they're kind of afraid of us. They still can't figure out where those letter *C's* came from. But they know we had something to do with it."

Carlos grinned back. "I think we've got it under control," he agreed.

They gave each other a high five.

"Gotcha!" they yelled together.

If you liked this book, you might enjoy these other titles by Margo Sorenson.

ॐ

Danger Canyon

Don't Bug Me

Firewatch

The Gotcha Plot

The Hidden Dagger

Kimo and the Secret Waves

Nothing Is for Free

Soccer Blaster

Time Trap

Who Stole the Bases?

ॐ

Available from Perfection Learning® Corporation